DATE DUE

LAWRENCE HIGH YEARBOOK SERIES
BOOK IV

COWBOY COOL

DAVID A. POULSEN

KEY PORTER BOOKS

Library and Archives Canada Cataloguing in Publication

Poulsen, David A., 1946-
    Cowboy cool / David A. Poulsen.

(Lawrence High yearbook series ; 4)
Originally published: Red Deer, Alta. : Coolreading.com, 2001.
ISBN 978-1-55470-099-8

    I. Title. II. Series: Poulsen, David A., 1946- . Lawrence High .
yearbook series ; 4.

PS8581.O848C58 2008   jC813'.54   C2008-902208-4

The publisher gratefully acknowledges the support of the Canada Council for the Arts and the Ontario Arts Council for its publishing program. We acknowledge the support of the Government of Ontario through the Ontario Media Development Corporation's Ontario Book Initiative.

We acknowledge the financial support of the Government of Canada through the Book Publishing Industry Development Program (BPIDP) for our publishing activities.

Key Porter Books Limited
Six Adelaide Street East, Tenth Floor
Toronto, Ontario
Canada M5C 1H6

www.keyporter.com

Text design: Marjike Friesen
Electronic formatting: Alison Carr

Printed and bound in Canada

08 09 10 11 12 5 4 3 2 1

For Spencer

1

It was the first pep rally of the year, and it had the usual stuff. First our Students' Union President, Arlene Mitchell, gave a little speech—one of those "rah-rah, be true to your school" things. Then the coaches went on stage and introduced their players.

We started with football. All the guys had their jerseys on as Coach K.Y. Briggs brought them out on stage. Since we're the defending city champions, there were some pretty big cheers, especially for French and Wild Thing. Those aren't their real names—they're actually Marcel Boileau and W.T. Zahara—but everybody knows them as French and Wild Thing. Maybe you know about them too. They were written up in the newspaper and in last year's Lawrence High School Yearbook. They were the heroes of the championship game.

Next came the baseball teams, then basketball, and so on. It was kind of fun. Some of the teams did skits, a couple were air bands—Arlene Mitchell, Pam Parlee, and Annette Difolia were the Dixie Chicks. They were awesome, even though a lot of kids didn't know who the Dixie Chicks were. Or what the song "Earl" was all about.

That's because Lawrence High is pretty much a rock school. Most of the kids like alternative, or rap, or fairly heavy metal. There aren't a lot of country music fans kicking around.

The other thing about Lawrence High is that we're a sports school. Kids at other schools call us the "jock joint," which is a pretty accurate description. Just about every sport you can name is played at Lawrence, and in every one of those sports, we have some of the best athletes in the city.

Yeah, just about every sport you can name— and a couple you and I might not think of. That's why we all got a big surprise when Miss MacDonald went up on stage. She teaches English and computers and I didn't know she had an interest in any sports at all. Anyway, when she got up there, she went to the microphone with this little smile on her face. You know, the smile teachers get when they know something you don't.

"Hello, Lawrence students," she said. "As you know, our team name is the Cowboys, but as far as I know, we've never had a real cowboy here. Well, I'd like you to meet a new student at Lawrence. He's the very first member of the Lawrence High School Rodeo Team. Please welcome a Lawrence High Cowboy and a real cowboy—bull rider Kelly Parker."

2

There wasn't much applause right away. Kelly Parker walked out on stage wearing his cowboy hat and a belt buckle the size of a garbage can lid. A few people laughed, and there was a lot of looking at each other and eye-rolling going on. But when Arlene started applauding and Wild Thing went over and high-fived the guy, the rest of us joined in and gave the bull rider a hand.

I'd never seen a bull rider up close before. When Kelly Parker smiled at the audience, I was surprised to see that he had a full set of teeth. Of course, I couldn't tell if they were real or not, but at least there weren't a lot of spaces where teeth are supposed to be.

I'd seen the guy around the halls some. I knew he was in grade ten, same as me, but the only class we had together was computers. And we were at opposite ends of the lab, so I hadn't paid much attention to him. I was paying attention now. He was standing there trying to look cool—which, if you ask me, is pretty hard to do in a cowboy hat and boots.

Miss MacDonald waved him over to the microphone. At first he shook his head, but then he walked over, leaned down and said, "Howdy" into the mike.

Personally, I thought the guy was a joke, but as I looked around the gym I could tell quite a few of the girls didn't agree. A lot of them were staring up at the stage like it was Keith Urban up there, not some local bull rider. I could see some of the guys were thinking about the same way I was— *yippee ding*, a cowboy.

Who knew if the guy was even any good? Anybody can say they ride bulls, but wearing a hat and having a hubcap stuck to your belly button doesn't make you a *real* cowboy. I doubt if Miss MacDonald would know a real cowboy from a ham sandwich.

Denny Hillman, who is about the biggest and strongest guy in the school, yelled, "Howdy!" back at the guy in this real high voice. Denny was already on stage with the football team. We all heard his "howdy," and everybody laughed like crazy. Well, not everybody. Miss MacDonald didn't laugh. And the girls who were ga-ga over the guy didn't laugh. And Wild Thing didn't laugh.

He went over and said something to Kelly Parker and Kelly said something back. Then Wild Thing walked up to the mike. He took it off the stand and turned to look at Denny. Wild Thing was in a band called The Heavy Breathers, so he knew how to handle a microphone. When he arrived at Lawrence the year before, he and Denny had quite a feud going. They're best friends now, but things were a little tense for a while. Actually, Denny's a good guy—he just tries to be funny all the time, and sometimes he doesn't quite pull it off.

Wild Thing looked right at Denny. "Hey, Meat," he said, "Kelly here has bull riding practice every Wednesday at a place a couple of miles out of town. He just told me he'd be happy to take you along and let you climb on a couple of those bulls if you'd like to try it. What do you say?"

Like I said, W.T. and Denny hadn't hit it off real good at first, and one of the things I remember most about their feud is how Wild Thing used to call Denny "Meat" all the time. Denny didn't like it then, and he didn't like it now. I could see the grin on his face turn sour. He got red too, and looked at the floor.

Then Wild Thing looked out at the audience. "Now what do you say we give the new guy a REAL Lawrence welcome!"

The applause was louder then and there was a little cheering, but it didn't look to me like the whole school was as ga-ga about the bull rider kid as those girls were. And they were probably just niners anyway.

I pulled out my MP3 player, put the earphones over my ears and let myself get into some Arcade Fire.

3

By the way, my name is Alex Borden. I'm not one of the athlete types, so right away you wonder what I'm doing at a school like Lawrence. It's simple really—I love sports as much as any kid going to this school. But I figured out a long time ago that a job on the playing field—any field—wasn't going to happen. You won't find me in the football team picture—too scrawny. Or the basketball team picture—too short. Or baseball—even with my glasses on I can't see well enough to hit a forty mile per hour fastball. I'm too slow for hockey, too clumsy for volleyball, and too soft for wrestling. I'm sure you get the picture.

With my glasses on, you could say I'm a

blonder version of Harry Potter. Except Harry has a better nose and no zits. I guess I do sort of look like somebody called "Brain," which I figure is better than looking like somebody called "Brawn."

That brings me back to what I'm doing at Lawrence High. I made up my mind a long time ago that I want a career in sports management. The funny thing is I've probably got a better chance of actually making a living in sports than most of the athletes. Maybe about one in five hundred of these jocks will actually suit up with a pro sports team. I figure my odds of landing some kind of sports position are a whole lot better than that.

And I'm getting lots of experience here at Lawrence. I'm the manager of the football team; trainer for both the boys and girls basketball teams; and official statistician for the baseball team. I think I've got a pretty good chance of getting a scholarship to a university, and maybe working for a couple of the sports teams there as well.

The other thing I guess you should know about me is that I'm a computer geek. Actually I hate that term, but the same kids who call me

"Brain" like to say that's what I am. And I guess it's sort of true—I am pretty good with computers.

None of the players on any of the teams call me "Brain," because they know I don't like it. And I guess maybe they realize that what I do for Lawrence teams is pretty important too. Kids on all the different teams are always coming to me and asking for a certain piece of equipment, or an update on their scoring stats. I'm used to requests from people, but I wasn't ready at all when the bull rider—Kelly Parker—came up to me right after English the next day.

"Hey, Alex," he said, "can I talk to you for a minute?"

"Uh ... yeah, I guess so," I said. "I've got a spare right now, but I need to go down to the gym and start laying out stuff for football practice." I figured he probably wanted some help with the English essay Mr. White had just assigned. The topic was "In *To Kill a Mockingbird*, is Atticus Finch a good dad or a bad dad?" I figured Kelly was one of those guys who wouldn't read the book, and would try to wing it on the essay. Unless he could get somebody like me to help him.

"No worries," Kelly smiled at me. "If you want, I can come and give you a hand."

"That's okay," I shook my head. I don't know why I didn't want him helping me. I guess the stuff I do in sports is my thing, and I just don't want to share it with anybody.

Kelly didn't push it, and I found myself sort of liking the guy. I mean, it wasn't his fault Miss MacDonald dragged him up on stage at the pep rally. And wanting help on an essay wasn't exactly a capital offence. Kids asked me for help all the time.

"We could go to the caf for a couple of minutes if you want," I said.

"Sure," he nodded.

When we got down there, I grabbed a Coke and Kelly got a coffee. He didn't offer to pay for mine, which I thought was strange considering the guy was about to ask for a favor. I'd expected him to suck up a little bit, at least.

When we sat down, he took a couple of sips of coffee, but didn't say anything.

I didn't have all day, so I figured I'd better get the conversation going. "I won't write your essay for you, but if you want to talk about some ideas, I can do that."

"What are you talking about?" He looked at me like I had three ears.

"Isn't that what you wanted to talk about—the English essay on *To Kill a Mockingbird*?"

Kelly laughed. He laughed hard, and for quite a long time. "That isn't it at all," he said finally. "I've got a business proposition for you."

4

That one almost floored me. I took a long drink of Coke. "What kind of business proposition?"

"Well, I guess you know that I rodeo."

"Uh-huh," I nodded.

"And I've heard you're some kind of computer genius."

I didn't exactly nod this time, but I didn't disagree either.

"Well, I've been thinking." Kelly set his coffee down and turned his chair to face me. "You know anything about bull riding?"

"I know there's a cowboy and a bull and the guy's supposed to ride for eight seconds," I told him. "That's about it."

"That's a good start." He grinned at me. "The thing is, bull riders like to know as much about the bulls they're about to get on as they can. At every rodeo and Bull Riding event, the bulls are drawn a few days ahead. If the rider hasn't been on that bull before, or he doesn't know the bull, he starts phoning around to ask other guys what they know."

"Why?"

"A lot of the bulls have a set pattern. Maybe they'll spin one direction or the other, or maybe they're real high jumpers—whatever. If you know what they're likely to do, your chances are a little better of staying on for that eight seconds."

"You mean these guys study the bulls like a hitter studies pitchers, or a goalie studies the shooters?" I was having a little trouble with that one. Rodeo didn't strike me as the most scientific of sports.

"That's exactly right," Kelly nodded. "Of course, animals aren't quite as predictable as baseball pitchers. Sometimes they'll mess you up and do something totally different from their regular pattern. But most of the time, they pretty well stick to the program."

"That's something I bet a lot of people don't know."

"Probably not," Kelly agreed. "Anyway, here's my idea. We start a computer program to keep track of the bulls. Every time they buck, we find out what they did, then we enter it into the computer and bingo, somebody wants to know about a bull, they phone us up and we email them the information, or they can look it up on our website."

"Are you telling me cowboys have computers?"

"Yep," Kelly nodded. "And cellphones. A lot of 'em have their own web pages too ... especially the top pro guys."

"And you think they'd want this info?"

"I know they would," Kelly said. "Not only that, they'd pay for it too. It's good for them because they wouldn't have to chase all over the country trying to find somebody who had ridden the bull recently. They just come to us—Buckers.com. What do you think?"

"I think it's a great idea," I told him. "I can design a web page for us. And I can even work up a program that will give us probabilities."

"What's that?" Kelly looked doubtful.

"You said the bulls usually do the same thing, but not every time. I can give a percentage that says 90 per cent of the time this bull spins to the right, but the other 10 per cent of the time he does something different."

Kelly looked impressed. "Cool. That would be really helpful."

"There's only one problem," I said. "How do we get the information? You can't be at every rodeo or Bull Riding event."

"I've got it covered," Kelly agreed. "We hire guys. At every event, I get a guy to make a few notes and phone 'em in to us. They all watch the bulls anyway. Then we give that guy free access to the service for so many events—say, the next three. That's how he gets paid."

"Not bad," I said. "But how do *we* get paid?"

"We send out bills once a month. You used Buckers.com four times this month. You owe us $40.00."

"Will they pay?"

"Oh, they'll pay," Kelly said. "And if they don't, we just cut off their service. They'll find out real fast that dealing with us makes a lot more sense than making half a dozen long distance calls for every bull they draw."

I could see Kelly had been giving this a lot of thought. Problem was, I was busy with all my other sports commitments. I probably would have said no if I hadn't remembered that my dad had phoned the other night. He lives right near Phoenix and the Super Bowl is being played there next year. Dad said he'd get us tickets if I saved up and paid for my own plane ticket ... this rodeo/Bull Riding thing could be my trip to the Super Bowl.

"I have to admit the idea sounds pretty good. How do we get started?"

Kelly pulled a worn notebook out of his back-pack. "I've already gathered up a lot of stats. I started in the spring. Once you can get this on the computer, I'll start promoting the idea with the bull riders and it won't be long before we find out if it's as popular as I think it's going to be."

"I'll start tonight," I said. "Let's get together in a few days and I'll let you know how it's going."

Kelly stuck out his hand. I wasn't used to shaking hands. High fives and stuff like that was what we did around Lawrence. But I figured shaking hands was what cowboys did. So we shook.

"And one more thing—it's your computer—you're going to have to input stuff and send out the e-mails so I think you should get 60 per cent of what we make. That okay with you … partner?"

"Sounds good … partner."

Kelly took off down the hall, then stopped and looked back at me. "Oh, and I'll make you a little bet."

"Yeah, about what?"

"That I beat you on the English essay." He was grinning at me.

"You mean get a better mark than me?"

"That's it."

"You're on." I felt a little bad taking the bet. *To Kill a Mockingbird* is one of my favorite books. I've read it three times. Not only that, but I can write pretty decent essays; better than a bull rider for sure. "You can dig into your share of the profits from Buckers.com to pay me."

He was still grinning as he headed off down the hall. *A lot of confidence for somebody who doesn't have a chance*, I thought to myself.

5

He beat me by 4 per cent—86 to 82 per cent. And when I talked to him about it afterward, he really knew the book backwards and forwards. So much for cowboys being illiterate. I have to admit that's kind of what I thought before Kelly showed up at our school.

Anyway, the essay marks weren't the big news at school. That honor belonged to the Devil's Platoon. The Platoon is about the worst gang around—not the kind of people parents want their daughters—or sons—associating with.

The Devil's Platoon are also bad news. They've had a feud going with Lawrence, and last year they showed up at a dance and started a fight with some of the students and Mr. White, our English teacher. Then later, they got Marcel Boileau—we call him French because he's from Quebec—by himself and put him in the hospital. Then they did the same thing to Mr. White. A couple of Platoon creeps wound up in the Young Offenders' Centre. Everybody at Lawrence knew that wouldn't be the end of it, and it turns out we were right. One night a couple of weeks after the pep rally, there was a red spray paint warning on one wall of the school, out by the smoking area.

It was in real big letters and it said, "Hey, Lawrence, we're back and we'll be seeing you … soon." All of us knew exactly who the painters were. Some of the kids at school freaked when they saw the sign. Especially French. I heard he didn't want to walk home by himself and I didn't blame him. I remember what his face looked like after the Platoon had got him the last time.

Personally, I thought it was probably just a threat to scare us, and that nothing more would happen. But maybe that was just wishful thinking. Anyway, it wasn't something I had to worry about. The Platoon didn't even know I was alive. And I planned to keep it that way.

Oh, yeah. There was one other newsworthy event at school at about that same time. Gail Banert spoke to me. I mean, it wasn't a big speech, but just knowing that Gail Banert was aware that we shared the same planet was huge. Gail is in my Com Tech class. She's probably the only person in the class that hasn't asked me for help.

It's not that Gail Banert is moviestar good-looking or anything. In fact, what I like about her is that she's kind of ordinary looking ... well sort of cute-ordinary. She's a little shorter than me, which isn't something you can say about a lot of girls. She has brown hair that I would call medium length and eyes about the same colour as her hair. Gail's eyes are definitely one of her best features. When she's looking at you, you can't help looking back just to get a better look at the eyes. At least that's how they affect me.

Not that Gail spends a lot of time looking at me. Plus I had her figured as kind of shy, which is not a good thing. It means that the first move is up to me. Historically, that has been a problem. The last girl I liked was in my grade six class. It took me three years to work up the courage to talk to her. And when I did it was to say "goodbye Cindy" on her last day at the school. The next day she and her family moved to San Antonio, Texas.

Anyway, what Gail Banert said to me was, "Excuse me, I need to get into my locker." I was sitting in front of it, reading the second part of *The Lord of the Rings*. I honestly didn't know it was her locker. And okay, maybe what she said wasn't exactly romantic, but it was conversation, and it was directed at me. I figured it wasn't a bad first step.

I guess it would have been better if I'd actually said something back. Something like, "Oh, sure … sorry." But I didn't. I just closed my book, stuffed it in my backpack, and got out of the way. I sort of smiled at her but she wasn't looking.

I'll say one thing about Kelly Parker—when he said he was going to do something, he did it. By the end of the second week after we had formed Buckers.com, he had reports from three more rodeos and one PBR Bull Riding for me to input. And he had eight bull riders already signed up. On Friday, he came up to me after English. I hadn't seen him coming because I was sort of looking up and down the halls hoping to catch a glimpse of Gail.

"How's it going getting that stuff into the computer?" he asked.

"Pretty good," I told him as I gave up my Gail-search. "I've got one more rodeo to input and I'll be caught up."

"Great," he nodded. "I'll have some more for you after this weekend. And I'm pretty sure I'll get some more guys signed up as well. Another few weeks, and we should be able to start providing the service."

I was thinking about the fact that Kelly talked more like a businessman than a bull rider—"providing the service"—but I didn't say anything.

"By the way," he said, "I've got a rodeo not far from here this Saturday. Feel like coming along? It'll give you a chance to see what your business partner actually does."

"Yeah," I told him. "That would be cool. I've

only been to one rodeo in my life, and I was pretty small then, so I hardly remember it."

"Great, I'll pick you up Saturday morning. It's an afternoon performance, so I'll have time to show you around some. If you're going to make money from this sport, you need to know something about it."

"No problem, just keep me away from the bulls," I said.

"Actually, I'll get you nice and close." He laughed. "You might as well get a bird's-eye view of what we do."

"Uh … okay." I wasn't sure about the bird's-eye view part.

6

That Saturday was memorable to say the least. For several reasons. The rodeo was incredible. It's one thing to see a rodeo from a grandstand on the other side of the arena—it's a totally different thing to be behind the chutes and right on top of all the action.

The rodeo started with bareback riding. That's where cowboys ride bucking horses without saddles. All they have to hang on to is a bareback rigging, which is a rawhide handle attached to a leather pad and strapped onto the horse. That handhold, the seat of their pants, and the heels of their boots is all the contact the riders have with the horses. And when you're as close to the action as I was, you see how hard those horses buck.

Next came the calf roping, which I didn't like much. "Not a lot of city people like this event," Kelly said, as I cheered when a roper missed his calf, and it ran off down the arena.

Then there was saddle bronc riding. I loved that event. Cowboys rode in saddles that had been modified. The horses jumped high, and then kicked out their back legs. It was pretty spectacular. This time, I cheered for the cowboys. Some guys rode and some guys didn't, and one had a score of eighty-four points on a horse called Bear Trap. Kelly told me any mark in the eighties was very good. The judges give half the points for the cowboy's ride, and half for the bucking horse. Kelly explained that it's the same with the bull riding, which is why the bull the guy draws is so important.

The next event was steer wrestling. Big guys—the kind you'd like on your offensive line—jump down off horses onto steers that are running full out. The guy has to stop the steer and twist him down onto the ground. The steers looked awful big to me, which I guess is why the guys doing the wrestling were the biggest in the rodeo.

Then it was time for ladies barrel racing. Now that was cool. Ladies and some young girls as well, raced in a cloverleaf pattern around barrels at top speed. The downer was the girl I was cheering for—mostly because she was seventeen and gorgeous—knocked over a barrel. When that happens, there's a five second penalty, and that pretty well ends her chances of winning anything.

Everything was happening so fast, I didn't have time to get bored. Suddenly, it was time for the bull riding. The stock contractor and his crew ran the bulls that would be bucked that day into the chutes. Some were so big, they barely fit in the chutes. Some stood quietly while others were throwing their heads and stomping and snorting. I was hoping Kelly had drawn one of the quiet ones.

He hadn't. His bull was called Bad Medicine, and Bad Medicine didn't look like he was in a good mood. I was about to get out of the way when Kelly grabbed me and said, "Come on, you're going to help me get on."

"Are you kidding? No way," I said.

"They can't hurt you where you'll be standing. Hurry up, there are only two guys ahead of me." I climbed up on the back of the chute where Bad Medicine was standing, still acting grumpy. Kelly and another cowboy passed the tail of Kelly's bull rope around the belly of the bull and looped it so that the handhold was facing up. Kelly climbed down on the back of the bull. Bad Medicine tried to turn his head to get a look at the guy he was going to try to dump on the ground, but he couldn't get his head totally around. I was glad about that.

Kelly took the tail of the rope and handed it to me. "Here hold this," he said. "Higher … that's it … now hold tight."

Kelly had already put resin on his bull rope and now ran his gloved hand up and down the rope to work the resin in. "Warming up the rope," was what he called it.

Then he put his hand into the handhold and told me to pull the rope as hard as I could. When I had it as tight as I could get it, Kelly took the tail of the rope and placed it into the palm of his hand across the top of the handhold. Then he worked the rest of the rope's tail around behind his wrist and into the palm of his hand one more time.

It looked awkward to me. It also looked like it would be hard for Kelly to let go if he got thrown off, or if he wanted to get off at the end of the eight seconds. I looked out into the arena. There were two rodeo clowns. One was a bullfighter whose main job was to help the cowboy escape from the bull when the ride was over. The other guy was called the barrel man. He stood in a huge red barrel, telling jokes and exchanging hilarious insults with the rodeo announcer. The clown and the announcer pretended to be mad at each other, but Kelly had told me they were best friends.

But there were no jokes now. Everyone's eyes were on chute number four where Kelly Parker was about to emerge on Bad Medicine. Kelly looked ready. He had slid up toward the front of the bull's body, so he was practically sitting on top of the handhold. He nodded his head and I heard him say, "Let's go, men," The guys on the ground swung the chute gate open and scrambled out of the way.

7

The bull turned and jumped all in one motion. I couldn't believe the power. I also couldn't believe how something that big could be so athletic. Kelly got tipped to one side as the bull came down hard on its front legs, with its back legs high in the air behind. In a way, it looked like Bad Medicine was standing on his head.

He didn't stay that way for long. As Kelly fought his way back into the middle of the bull's broad back, Bad Medicine jumped high again. This time, when his front feet hit the ground, he started a turn to the right. It was only a quarter turn, so he wasn't really spinning. His next jump wasn't as high, and for the rest of the eight seconds, he jumped and turned, but none of the moves were as tough as the first couple.

Kelly handled the rest of the ride pretty easily. With the help of the bullfighter who distracted the bull, Kelly was able to get off and back to the chutes without a problem.

"Awright!" I shouted. "That was awesome."

Kelly was shaking his head. "He didn't have a real good day. Most of the time he spins a lot harder than that. My score won't be all that great."

He was right. "The score for Kelly Parker," the announcer told the crowd, "is seventy-six points."

I figured if eighty was a good score, seventy-six couldn't be all that bad. And it wasn't. It just wasn't good enough to win money at that rodeo. There had already been two scores in the eighties the day before. The last bull rider was the Canadian Champion, and he rode his bull to an eighty-five. He was the leader.

Kelly explained that only the top six guys won money. Kelly was sitting sixth after the first two days of the rodeo. If even only one guy scored more than seventy-six on Sunday, Kelly wouldn't place. He didn't seem all that upset though, and after a little while he was pretty well back to his normal self. For the first couple of minutes after the ride, he had been pretty psyched up. It didn't surprise me that it took time to come down after something like that. I figured it would take about three days for me to come down if I ever did what Kelly had just done.

The rodeo was over for the day. But before we left, we visited with people behind the chutes. Kelly introduced me to a lot of guys, and a couple even asked how Buckers.com was coming along.

"Great," I told them. "Should have our first data ready to be accessed in the next week or so."

It had been a good day so far. I liked the rodeo even more than I thought I would and it looked like our little business was about to take off. But things were about to take a turn for the worse. We got out to the parking lot, and were about to get into Kelly's truck—a big black Dodge with a Cummins Diesel—when I heard someone yell, "Hey, Kelly."

Three members of the Devil's Platoon were leaning against a muscle car I'd never seen before. As we stopped and stared, they started coming our way.

"Let's get out of here," I said.

"No, it's okay, nothing to worry about."

"Are you kidding me?" They were getting closer. "Do you know who those guys are?"

Kelly slapped me on the shoulder. "I said there's nothing to worry about. You stay here. I'll be right back."

He walked toward them. They met a little too far away for me to hear what they were saying, but the weird thing was, there was a lot of laughing, and what looked like friendly talk happening. I couldn't believe it. One of the Platoon guys and Kelly exchanged high fives like they were long-lost pals.

After a couple of minutes, Kelly came back to the truck. "Okay, let's go," he said.

I didn't move. "Are you friends with those losers?"

"I know a couple of them from my old school, that's all."

"It looked like more than that to me," I said.

"Look, Alex, just leave it alone. I said I know a couple of those guys and that's the end of it, all right?"

As we were getting into the truck, one of the Platoon guys yelled, "Don't forget, man."

Kelly yelled back, "I'll handle it, okay?"

And that was it. We didn't talk much as Kelly drove me home. I didn't feel like talking any more. Suddenly, Kelly Parker wasn't the cool kid from school. He wasn't even the bull riding cowboy I'd watched that afternoon. This was a different Kelly, one I didn't like. Not at all.

8

The thing I like best about being fifteen is that even when you have a really lousy day, there's a pretty good chance the next one will be okay. Maybe even excellent.

Well, that's the way it was after the day at the rodeo. Except that it was actually two days later that things turned incredibly cool. That was the day Gail Banert spoke to me again. And this time she did more than ask me to get out of her way.

It happened at Shakey's Pizza and Ginger Beef Garage, which is pretty much the Lawrence High hangout. It's a great spot, and you can go there almost any time of the day or night and see somebody you know.

I was sitting with Curt Tomlinson and his girlfriend Judy Baird. They hooked up last year. Curt has one of the coolest cars at Lawrence—a '58 Meteor. What's kind of neat is that Judy and Curt work on the car together. I guess it's no big deal for a couple to work on a car together, except that in this case Judy Baird is blind. As in, almost totally. But Curt talks to her and tells her where stuff is under the hood, and once she finds something, there isn't much she can't fix.

Of course, they told me all about the car and how Curt was doing in his tryout with the Canucks Junior Hockey Team. I wasn't saying much. I think maybe my mind was still on the rodeo and what had happened in the parking lot after. I was about to ask Curt and Judy what they thought of the whole thing, but I didn't get the chance.

Just then, Gail Banert slid into the booth. She slid in *next to me*. My mouth got really dry, and I had to take a giant drink of Coke before I could even say "hi."

Gail and Judy are friends, and they did some major chick-visiting, while Curt and I watched in silence. I was okay with that, because it meant I didn't have to think up something to say.

Then, just about the time I figured I wouldn't have to say anything at all, they stopped talking and Gail looked at me. I think she even leaned toward me a little, but maybe that was wishful thinking.

"I've been wanting to talk to you, Alex," she said.

"Oh ... uh ... yeah? I've been wanting to talk to you too." *Now what did I say that for?*

"Oh, well you go first then," Gail smiled. "What did you want?"

"Want? Oh ... uh ... nothing really. I just ..." *How was I going to get out of this? I couldn't tell her that what I wanted was for us to get married or at least engaged.* "Uh ... no nothing ... really." *Great cover, Alex.*

I could hear a kid in the booth behind me laughing hysterically.

"Did somebody already tell you?" Gail put her hand on my arm.

"Tell me what?"

"About the committee." She took her hand

away. I was wishing she hadn't done that. I liked the feel of it on my arm.

"Committee?"

"Yeah, I'm chairing a committee on what our school should be doing to make it a better place for students to be. It's called 'The Next Five Years. How Can We Be Better?' We shortened it to the '5 2 B Better Committee.' I was wondering if you'd like to be on it. We're going to have meetings every Thursday at noon in the biology lab."

The kid in the booth behind leaned over into our booth. I'd seen him around, but I didn't know his name. He was an eleventh grader. "You want 'Brain' on your committee? That should pretty well put everybody to sleep."

"No," Gail said. "I want *Alex* on my committee. He's got really good ideas, and he'd be great."

"Why don't you take me instead? I'll show you a couple of ideas of my own."

"Hey, Powell," Curt grinned at the mouthy kid, "take a bite of hamburger. If you're eating you're not talking, and if you're not talking you sound a lot smarter."

The kid threw a napkin at Curt and slid back into his own booth. "Greg Powell," Curt explained to the rest of us. "He's all right. Just thinks he's a comedian."

"So how about it, Alex?" Gail asked again. "Will you be on the committee?"

"Well ... yeah, okay ... sure ... if you think ..."

I didn't finish, because Gail hugged me. Right there in Shakey's, *Gail Banert hugged me*.

"See you next Thursday at noon," she said and slid back out of the booth. "See you, Curt. See you, Judy." She walked over to another booth where Arlene Mitchell and Brad Murray were sharing a milkshake—you know one shake, two straws. Jeez, I thought that stuff went out in the fifties.

There was another guy in the booth too. I didn't recognize him, but I was hoping he wasn't Gail's boyfriend.

"Hey, Alex," Curt leaned forward. "You have a very red face, Dude. If I didn't know better, I could get the idea that you think Gail is hot."

"Yeah," Judy laughed. "It's so bright in here, it's even bothering my eyes."

"Do you guys think … uh … do you … aw, forget it. I should get going," I said.

"Actually, Alex," Curt said, "I do think, but you're going to have to ask her out. That's all there is to it."

"Yeah, I know but …"

"It's perfect," Judy said. "You can tell her you've got a few ideas for the 5 2 B Better Committee, but you'd like to run them by her first. Then you say, 'So maybe we should catch a movie, and then we'll go to Shakey's and I'll tell you all about my ideas.'"

"You think that would work?"

"Can't fail," Judy nodded.

"But I don't have any ideas for the committee. I just found out about it five minutes ago."

"Then come up with some. We can't do everything for you," Judy laughed.

"Besides, anyone can see the woman's nuts about you," Curt added.

"Yeah, right." I was having a little trouble with that. "Anyway, thanks for the tip. Maybe I'll try it." I stood up.

"Don't wimp out, Alex," Curt said. "Just ask

her and everything will be fine."

"See you guys." I started for the door.

I was almost there, when I suddenly found a real good reason to stop. The door of Shakey's opened, and in walked a couple of members of the Devil's Platoon. In all the times I'd been in Shakey's, I'd never seen any of the Platoon in there. And coming through the door right behind them was Kelly Parker.

9

Kelly didn't look much like a cowboy right at that moment. He was wearing a black leather jacket, and looked like he'd just climbed off a Harley. He grinned when he saw me, but it didn't look all that natural. I got the feeling he was wishing I wasn't there.

"Hello, Alex," he said as the three of them walked by. I didn't bother to answer.

They sat in a booth in a corner, and for a second I thought maybe everything would be okay. I don't know why, but I decided not to leave. I went and sat back down with Curt and Judy. I could see Curt was telling Judy about the new arrivals.

"Things might just get a little interesting, Alex," Curt said.

"Maybe they're just going to have a shake or something and leave," I said hopefully. "I mean, they have as much right to be here as anybody."

"Are you forgetting what they spray-painted on the wall at school?" Judy reminded me. To tell the truth, I had forgotten.

"And it was Lawrence students who got them sent to juvie for a while," Curt added.

I nodded, and looked over at the booth in the corner. They were just talking to each other, waiting for whatever they'd ordered to arrive. Then, just about the time I started to get my hopes up that we might get through the evening without any trouble, one of the Platoon guys turned in the booth and said in a very loud voice, "Lawrence sucks ... and I'll bet there isn't anybody in this place that's gonna argue with me."

For a minute it looked like nobody would. Curt is a hockey player and a pretty tough guy, and I could see he was all for telling the guy to shut his face. But Judy was squeezing his arm and whispering. "It's not worth it, Curt. Even if you cleaned all three of them, they'd be back with six more the next time."

Curt relaxed a little, and once again I thought we'd be okay. That's when a voice I didn't expect to hear spoke up. "Why don't you idiots get a life?" The voice belonged to Gail Banert.

I looked over, and there she was on her feet, staring straight at the Platoon guys. For a moment, it went totally quiet in Shakey's. Then the biggest Platoon creep eased out of the booth and stood up.

"Well, what do you know? There *is* somebody at Lawrence with some guts after all. 'Course, it's a girl, but then that's what Lawrence is, isn't it … a girls' school?"

Curt had had enough. He pulled his arm away from Judy and got out of the booth. "Why don't you blow it out…" Curt was walking towards the guy, and I'm not sure what would have happened if Shakey hadn't come out of the kitchen just then. He got between Curt and the Platoon guy.

Nobody knows a whole lot about Shakey, but nobody jerks him around. "Fun's over," he said. "You punks are out of here. Now." He pointed at the two Platoon guys and Kelly. "I said now!"

They started toward the door, but stopped before they went out. The big guy looked back at Curt. "I'm gonna remember you, Shooter. We'll be getting together again."

"Whatever," Curt said, which is about what you'd expect a guy to say in that situation.

After they were gone, Curt sat back down, and Shakey came over to our table. "Curt, you better be careful, and I don't just mean tonight. It's not worth messing with those guys."

"Yeah, I know."

I think Curt was starting to remember what had happened to French and to Mr. White the year before. I know I was. But mostly I was mad. And mostly I was mad at Kelly Parker. I didn't think he was an actual member of the Platoon, at least he didn't have one of their stupid crests on his jacket. The crest had three army guys marching side by side, and all three had Satan's face. Cute, real cute.

But if he wasn't in the gang, what was Kelly doing hanging out with those guys? That was the part I couldn't figure out. I decided right then and there to ask him the next time I saw him at school.

Shakey left, and Gail Banert came back to our booth. She slid in next to me again, but she was looking across the table. "Thanks, Curt, but you didn't have to do that. Now they're going to have it in for you."

The same thought had occurred to me, and I think Curt had figured it out too. He nodded, but I noticed he wasn't saying anything, and he was swallowing a lot. Still, he had stood up and defended the woman I love which, by rights, should have been my job. I was considering whether having Gail think I was a hero was worth dying for when the door opened again. Every head in the place snapped in that direction. I guess you could say we were spooked.

It wasn't the Platoon. It was Wild Thing and Denny Hillman. Pam Parlee was with Denny, and Wild Thing was by himself. That was hard to figure, because it seemed like about two thirds of the girls at Lawrence liked the guy. There was a rumor that he had a girlfriend, and that she was quite a bit older. But nobody seemed to know for sure.

They hadn't made it very far through the door

before half the people in the place were telling them what had happened. Denny and Wild Thing had gone nose to nose with the Platoon before, so if anybody knew what the gang was all about, those two did.

But even they weren't able to come up with any ideas about what Kelly Parker was doing with those guys. "What about you, Alex? You've been hanging out with Kelly. What's with him and the Platoon?"

"I don't know. I ... just don't know." It was true. I couldn't figure it out. But what was bothering me most was the conversation he'd had with the two Platoon guys in the parking lot after the rodeo. And worst of all was the last part of the conversation.

"*Don't forget, man,*" the Platoon guy had yelled. And Kelly had yelled back, "*I'll handle it.*" Handle what? I wasn't sure I wanted to know.

10

Life gets pretty weird sometimes. Let me give you an example. There's a door in the library of our school. No big deal, except that this door is about fifteen feet off the ground. It's in the wall right over Miss Weston's desk—she's the librarian. There are no stairs up to this door, and as far as anyone knows, it doesn't go anywhere. It's just there.

Lawrence is a really old school, and maybe the door actually had a purpose once. But now it just sits there, looking like something the original construction workers put there as a joke.

Last week, Miss Weston came up with an idea for a writing contest. Students were supposed to write a story about the door. Actually, it sounded like kind of a neat idea for a contest. The prize was going to be books (what a surprise!) and the winning story would be published in the year-book. But the kicker was that when you put your name in at the library, it would be paired up with someone else's. Then the two of you had to work together on the story. Miss Weston said it was so students could get to know each other better.

That night when I said my prayers, (yeah, I do, okay?) I added a special one. I figured it wouldn't hurt to put in the word that I'd like to be paired with Gail Banert.

It didn't work. But remember what I said about life being weird? The partner I did get was Kelly Parker. My first thought was to drop out of the contest, but I decided to wait until I finished telling him what a jerk I thought he was for hanging out with the Platoon.

I saw him in the hall right after the noon bell, and he came up to me like everything was totally normal. "Hey, Alex," he grinned at me, "isn't this wild? You and me—two of the best writers in the place. We should kick butt in that contest."

"Are you nuts?" I stared at him. "You think

I'm going to work with you? Get one of your Platoon buddies to help write the stupid story." I started walking away, and then turned back. "And forget our little business venture, too. I'm kind of particular about who I associate with. Maybe that's something you should try."

I headed off down the hall. Kelly caught up to me and grabbed my arm. He spun me around so I was staring straight into his face, and this time he wasn't grinning. "You shouldn't go spouting off about stuff you don't know anything about."

"I know all I need to know," I said.

"No, you don't, but it doesn't matter. You can stick your contest. Oh, and one more thing." He reached into his pocket and pulled out some money. "Sixty per cent of this is yours. This is the first payment from the guys who want in on Buckers.com. I'll just give it back to them. I'll tell them my partner didn't live up to his end of the deal."

That part got to me. I didn't care about the money—well, not that much. There'll be other Super Bowls ... yeah, right. But I've always hated it when anybody accused me of not doing what

I said I was going to do. That's just a thing with me.

This time Kelly had started off down the hall, and it was my turn to chase him. "Hold it," I said. "I said I'd do this, and I'll do it. You just keep getting the information, and I'll get it up on the web page. But that's it. No meetings, no chit-chat. I don't want anybody to think we're friends, because we're not."

"Fair enough," the corners of Kelly's mouth were turned up a little, like he was trying to keep from smiling. "And … uh … what about the contest? We could work the same way. No contact. I write the first half, you write the second half— something like that."

"Uh … I don't know."

"Yeah, I don't blame you," Kelly nodded. "I beat you on the *To Kill a Mockingbird* essay and you're probably thinking you won't be able to match my writing."

"You must have bumped your head. I could write a better story than you in my sleep."

"Yeah, right." The corners of his mouth were moving again.

"Go ahead," I said. "You write the first half of the story and I'll write the last half. And if we win, it'll be because my half was terrific."

"See you, Alex." He started off down the hall again, and this time I let him go. But there was still something bugging me. This conversation hadn't turned out at all like I wanted it to. Kelly Parker had pushed my buttons, and I ended up whipped like the family pig, as my weird Uncle Jim likes to say.

I got over it in a hurry. I had to. Today was the first meeting of the 5 2 B Better Committee. I got my lunch out of my locker and headed for the biology lab. That's where the meeting was taking place. If I couldn't have Gail for a writing partner, I'd just have to dazzle her with my brilliant contributions to the committee.

11

A biology lab isn't one of my favorite places. I admit I'm kind of squeamish about dead stuff. The only time I ever cheated in school was when I got Lois Mead to dissect my frog for me a couple of years ago, so I wasn't nuts about the meeting being there. But if Gail Banert was going to be there, they could have the meeting in a dumpster and I'd show up.

There were six people on the committee. I only knew one of them other than Gail—Annette Difolia. She was French's girlfriend, and very cute. She was also a good friend of Gail's, so I figured she'd be a good person to get to know.

There were some pretty good ideas brought

up at the meeting. Gail told us that each meeting would have a different theme to help focus our energy and ideas. The theme for this meeting was the school's appearance.

Partway through the meeting, I had an idea. "A good place to start would be the school sign. It's looking pretty bad."

"Great idea, Alex," Gail said, and there was a lot of nodding of heads around the table.

The sign has been out in front of the school for almost as long as there's been a school. It's kind of like a big billboard, except it's only about three feet off the ground and a lot of the paint has worn or peeled off. It's mostly an eyesore, and I've even heard some people say it should be torn down.

One thing I'll say about Gail Banert: She might be shy and kind of quiet, but she isn't one to put things off. By the time we left the meeting, she had a crew organized to paint the sign the next day after school. We decided on a gold background with the words "Go Cowboys Go" painted in blue. Blue and gold were our team colours. Annette, who is an excellent artist, would do the lettering.

Gail volunteered to get permission from the administration. Needless to say, I offered to help with the project, even though I'm maybe the worst artist on the planet.

"I think we should keep the whole thing a secret," Gail said. "Let's not tell anybody about it, and when everyone gets to school Wednesday morning it'll be a big surprise."

We all agreed that this was a good idea. So why did I blab to Kelly Parker the next day? I have no idea. Maybe I just wanted to impress him, or let him know that I wasn't totally dependent on him for my social life. Honestly, I don't have a clue. But that's what I did. When he walked up to me right outside the library with the first half of the story for the contest, I opened up like a can of tuna.

He didn't say much. Maybe he wasn't impressed, or maybe he just didn't care what I did when I wasn't helping him with Buckers.com. Anyway, he nodded and said he was sure I'd like his half of the story; then he left. Nothing like a little confidence.

The thing is, I *did* like his half of the story. It was all about a mysterious woman who'd been secretly living in the school for forty years. The door led to her room. Every day, when classes were on, she stayed hidden away, but at night she came out and wandered the halls.

And that's where Kelly ended his part of the story. It was up to me to write about *why* this woman had been squirrelled away in that place all these years. I was kind of looking forward to it, mostly because Kelly's part got my imagination working big time.

That evening, our work crew gathered for the painting. It was fun, although I think I would have done a better job if I'd spent more time looking at the sign and less looking at Gail. Even in really grubby painting clothes, Gail looked pretty great to me.

We were almost finished when Gail and I suddenly found ourselves alone by the paint tray. She was cleaning a couple of brushes and I was getting paint to do one last corner of the sign. I'm not sure what came over me exactly, but I did something I'd never done before. I asked a girl out. Sort of.

"So … uh … Gail…. I was wondering … uh …,

you want to go over to Shakey's after we finish and have a shake or something?"

"Well," she looked up at me from where she was kneeling down and cleaning brushes, "I have some things I have to do tonight—"

"Yeah, that's okay," I said really fast, "I know you're busy and everything—"

"So I can't stay long, but sure, I'd love to go."

"Serious?" I thought maybe she was putting me on.

"As long as you don't mind being seen with a girl looking like this." She gestured to indicate her grubby clothes.

"I think you look great like that." As soon as I said it I was afraid she might think I thought she looked better grubby than when she was neat and clean. I tried to fix it, but things went from bad to worse.

"I mean … you know … you look good without your paint clothes on too … uh … that's not what I meant. What I meant …"

Gail was laughing. "I know what you meant, Alex."

I just shook my head and laughed too.

When we finished the sign (I have to say it looked very cool) we headed over to Shakey's. Of course, some other people went too, but Gail went with me. We didn't do the one-shake-two-straws thing; in fact, Gail didn't do a shake at all. She's one of the school's healthier eaters, so she ordered a small diet coke. I had a chocolate shake.

But we talked lots—about all kinds of things. Right up until she said she had to go. Her mom came and picked her up, and as she went out the door, Gail Banert gave me a smile that turned my legs into Jell-O pudding. I figured life couldn't get much better.

That feeling lasted right up until I got to school the next morning. I could see a lot of kids gathered around the sign, and I wandered over to soak up some of the praise about how great it looked.

The only problem was, the sign looked a little different than the way we'd left it the night before.

Now it said, "Go Cowboys Go" in big blue letters, just the way Annette had painted it. But under that, in bright red, was scrawled, "Coming soon to your school—The Devil's Platoon!"

12

My first reaction was to blame our rotten luck. I mean, what are the chances that some Platoon jerk just happened to come along right after we finished our sign?

It wasn't long before that feeling went away. Of course, it was ridiculous to think that's what happened. Oh, and the Platoon guy just happened to have a can of spray paint with him. Yeah, right.

It didn't take me long to figure out just how the Platoon knew about the sign. They'd gotten the news from their good friend, Kelly Parker. And the part that made me really sick was that Kelly Parker had gotten the news from me.

I spent the day hating myself. I knew I couldn't

tell anyone—especially Gail—about my big mouth. But I also knew that I had to do something. And punching Kelly in the face wasn't the answer. All that would do is get me beat up ... maybe a couple of times.

I didn't have a very good day in the learning department. I can't remember any of Mr. White's English class. I was still in a fog in chemistry, and not much better in math. When noon rolled around, I didn't feel much like eating. Believe me, that's not like me. I'm not all that big, but I eat like a linebacker; at least that's what my dad says.

But not that day. I sat on the floor in the hall and stared at the locker across from me. I remember it was number 253. I think that was about the only piece of information that I actually took in that day.

But then one of those strange timing things happened. I was still staring at 253 when I heard a voice. Normally, that particular voice would have had me on my feet in a second, and fumbling to tuck in my shirt. The voice belonged to Gail Banert. That day, though, I was so depressed she had to say, "Hi, Alex" twice before it even registered.

I got up and looked at her. "Hi, Gail."

"I guess you saw the sign, huh?" she said.

I nodded. "I saw it."

"Well, it's no big deal. We've still got some blue paint. We'll just paint over the Platoon's little addition," she said.

"Yeah, but it kind of wrecked our big surprise," I pointed out. "Instead of seeing something really cool when they got to school, they saw that."

And that's when the strange timing moment happened. Kelly Parker came around the corner. He stopped when he saw us, and looked like he wanted to go the other way. Of course he couldn't, so instead he said, "Oh … uh … hi, guys."

"Hi, Kelly," Gail said.

I didn't say anything.

Gail looked at me and then at Kelly. "We … Alex and I … were wondering if you'd like to help us out with the sign. We have to repaint it. I guess you know why."

I thought she'd lost her mind. In the first place, I hadn't been wondering about Kelly helping us with the sign. As a matter of fact, I was pretty sure he had something to do with the sign being vandalized in the first place.

"Yeah, I ... uh ... saw it. I ... uh ... got some things to do ... after school." Kelly was mumbling and looking everywhere but at Gail or me. "Sorry," he started to walk away.

That was something else I didn't get. The guy looked really depressed. If he was as tight with the Platoon as I figured he was, he ought to have been proud of helping them out.

Just then, Denny and Pam came along. Pam had helped with the sign, too "Hey, Parker," Denny yelled.

Kelly turned around.

"The word is you're pretty good with spray paint," Denny said.

Kelly just looked at him. He didn't look scared. He just looked like he didn't care. To tell the truth, I had to admire him a little. Denny is easily the biggest kid in the school, not big as in fat—big as in ... big.

But Kelly didn't back down. He just stood there looking at Denny, almost like he was waiting to get hit. I couldn't figure out what he was doing. If I didn't know better, I'd have said he wanted Denny to hit him, but that didn't make sense. Bull riders might be tough, but I doubted they liked pain just for the fun of it.

"Somebody saw you last night. They said you spray-painted the sign, Rodeo Boy, and now you're going to pay the price." Denny took a step toward Kelly.

Still Kelly didn't move. So maybe Kelly figured he deserved it—sort of accepting his punishment. But the whole thing scared me. I was mad as hell at him, but if he didn't defend himself, he was going to get hurt—big time.

I jumped up. "It couldn't have been him," I said. "He was with me. We were working on our rodeo business last night at my place."

I don't know why I did it. I think if Kelly had given Denny attitude or taken a poke at him, I'd have let him get smacked. But there was something wrong with the way this whole thing was going down. I wasn't sure what it was, I just knew I didn't like it.

"That's crap, Brain, and you know it." Denny looked at me.

Pam took hold of Denny's arm. "Come on, Denny. You don't know for sure it was Kelly who wrecked the sign."

"Yeah, I do." Denny didn't look like he was about to walk away.

"Denny." Pam sounded pretty serious. "I'm going now. Are you coming with me?"

Denny looked at her. Pam had let go of his arm and she didn't look happy.

It was pretty obvious to all of us that Denny was going to have to choose between keeping his girlfriend and punching out Kelly. I guess Denny figured that out too, and he chose the girlfriend. Not a bad decision if you ask me, since Pam Parlee is one of the most awesome girls at Lawrence. Denny glared back at Kelly as they walked away.

One thing I'll say for Kelly. He still didn't look scared or even relieved. He started to walk away in the opposite direction from Denny and Pam. Then he stopped and turned back.

"If you guys still want help with that sign, I've got some time."

13

It didn't take long. Most of the Platoon's spray paint was below our letters, and only a couple of letters needed touching up. Kelly did most of the work.

He didn't say much, and didn't look at me, or even talk to me once. I couldn't tell if he was mad that I'd tried to help him with Denny or what.

We finished the sign and stood back to admire our work. It looked awesome. There were some high fives and some laughing, but the situation still felt a little tense. I guess we were wondering what the deal was with Kelly. There were times—times like this—when you figured the guy was completely cool. But if he was such a great guy, what was his connection with the Platoon?

I was working that one around in my mind
when a car came screeching up to the curb right
behind us. It was the same muscle car I'd seen at
the rodeo, and five guys from the Platoon jumped
out. I recognized two of them. I didn't know the
other three, but it was obvious one was the leader.
He did all the talking.

"Hey, Parker, been looking for you."

Kelly didn't answer.

"Get in, we got some things to talk about."
The leader of the Platoon didn't look like somebody I'd want to get to know.

Kelly took a small step forward. He didn't
look like he wanted to go.

"We're all going over to Shakey's, Kelly," Gail
said. "You're welcome to join us."

"Let's go, Parker ... now," the Platoon creep
barked.

"Hey, I'll even buy," I told Kelly.

"Shut up, will you?" The Platoon creep
looked at me and I hate to admit it, but I shivered.

Nobody said anything for a few seconds. I
could see Kelly was having a tough time making
up his mind. "Oh, I almost forgot," the Platoon

guy grinned at us. "Parker here has some work to do." He reached in to the car and pulled out a can of spray paint. "Yeah, Parker's quite the artist. Been doing a nice job with the spray paint lately. Well, Kelly, ol' pal, guess you'd better fix up that sign." He threw the spray paint can to Kelly who caught it but didn't move.

Kelly looked at Gail, then at me. It was awful quiet just then. Finally, Kelly looked back at the Platoon leader and threw the spray paint back to him. "I don't think so, Squeege."

My first thought was, *what kind of stupid name is Squeege?* My second thought was, *we're all going to die.*

That's when things took a turn for the better. Another car came screaming up behind the first one. This one was Curt Tomlinson's '58 Meteor, with Curt at the wheel. French was with him, and best of all, Denny was also in the car. All three of them got out in a hurry. Suddenly, the odds had improved a whole bunch. I stopped working on the obituary I'd been composing in my mind. Maybe we'd get out of this after all.

Pam, Judy, and French's girlfriend, Annette

got out of the car, too.

"What's happenin'?" Denny said, like he was asking about the weather.

"These jerks want Kelly to wreck our sign," Gail said. "He just finished telling them no way."

Denny looked at Kelly, with a little smile on his face. "Guess I was wrong about you."

"Not exactly," Kelly said. "I'm the one who's been spray-painting all the messages from the Platoon." He turned to where all the Platoon guys were lined up like gunfighters in a western movie. "But not this time."

It happened fast. Not being a fighter, I wasn't expecting things to just sort of explode. But they did. The Platoon all moved at the same time. The leader went for Denny. They'd had it out before— at the fight at the dance—and had come out about even. Squeege was as tall as Denny, but not as heavy. He was plenty tough, though.

Two more went after Curt and French, while the other two jumped Kelly. It took me a few seconds to figure out that what was happening was a brawl. It was a few more seconds until I figured out that Kelly was taking a pretty good beating, and that I'd have to get involved. Maybe it's a good thing everything was moving so fast. If I'd had more time to think, I might have decided to just go home and watch *The Simpsons*.

But I didn't. I jumped on the back of one of the guys that was giving it to Kelly. The guy flicked me off like I was a fly and went back at Kelly. I landed on the ground. Right next to me was an open can of Lawrence-gold paint. I grabbed it and jumped up. Just as the guy who'd tossed me off was about to take another punch at Kelly, I dumped the paint over his head.

It stopped him in his tracks. He was sputtering and trying to get the paint out of his eyes. He turned blindly toward me, and I did something I'd never done before in my life. I punched somebody.

Actually, I punched him pretty good. I connected right with his nose. Something I noticed is that a nose makes this squishing sound when you punch it. At least I think it was his nose. Or maybe it was the paint. Anyway, the guy went down and his fighting was over for the day.

I turned around and noticed that Kelly was doing fine with the other guy. Over by the sign,

Denny and Squeege were pummelling each other, but Denny had the edge, mostly because it would take a bus to actually knock him down. Curt was wailing on his guy, but French, who was even smaller than me, was having a rough time. Right up until Annette kicked the guy he was fighting in the shins, and Pam smacked him in the side of the head with her biology textbook. Suddenly I liked biology more than I ever had.

Just as quickly as it had started, the fight was over. It wasn't like in the movies, where all the bad guys are on the ground out cold. In this fight the bad guys were all still standing, except the one I'd painted and punched. But they didn't want to fight anymore.

Kelly's face was a mess of bruises and welts, but he didn't seem to care. Denny had a major welt over one eye, and a little blood around his mouth. Still, he looked a lot better than Squeege, who was having trouble seeing out of either eye.

French was puffy around one eye and his lips. I figured Annette would help with the lips' recovery. Curt and I came out of the scrap without much in the way of marks. Actually, I did have some evidence that I'd been in a fight. I had spilled some of the gold paint on my pants.

Speaking of paint … the Platoon was about to get one more surprise. While the fight had been going on, Gail hadn't been idle. She had taken the blue paint and a brush and painted "Lawrence rules!" on the hood of the muscle car.

It took the five of them some time to actually get over to the car and climb inside. I won't bother repeating the things they were saying as they drove off, but you can pretty well guess.

We all stood around looking at each other, not saying much, but grinning like crazy, even French through his sore lips. Finally Gail said, "I think it's time we did Shakey's."

No one disagreed.

14

I was the expert. That doesn't happen a whole lot in my life, but today I was the man.

The occasion was the high school rodeo in Rapid Falls, about an hour away. We'd filled a couple of cars and headed off to cheer on Lawrence's one rodeo competitor—Kelly Parker. We were in the bleachers wearing our Lawrence sweatshirts and cowboy hats. Some of the hats were pretty funny. They didn't look like the ones the real cowboys were wearing, but we didn't care.

Even Miss MacDonald was with us, and she was wearing the most ridiculous hat of all. Jeremy Van Pelt, who is a really excellent musician, had brought his violin along and played a couple of western polka-type tunes. We even danced in the bleachers. I don't think the other rodeo fans had seen that before.

A lot had happened in the three weeks since the big fight. A couple of teachers had seen what was happening and called the cops. They questioned us and then went after the guys in the Devil's Platoon. The cops found drugs in the car (nobody ever said Platoon members were smart) and arrested them all. The leader was back in the Young Offenders' Center and would be there for a while this time.

Kelly told us all about his connection with the Platoon while we were sitting at Shakey's after the fight. We'd all jammed into two side-by-side booths. By the way, Gail and I were drinking a strawberry shake—one strawberry shake and two straws.

Kelly was holding a cloth against his cheek, and he spent a lot of time looking down, like he was embarrassed or something. "I guess I sort of screwed up," he said.

Nobody said anything. I guess we all wanted to let him take his time.

"There was this girl. Her name was Julie."
Kelly was not a loud talker, but his voice was even
quieter than usual. "I met her at a rodeo dance. I
liked her quite a bit—actually, a lot—and I thought
she liked me okay. Anyway, a week or so later she
phoned me up and invited me to a party. I went,
and it turned out to be a Platoon party. Julie's
brother is in the Platoon."

Kelly took a deep breath and a drink of his Coke
float before he continued. "All I heard all night long
was how much the Platoon hated Lawrence, and
wanted to get even for what happened last year. I
wanted to impress Julie, so I talked like a hot shot
and said I could help them out a little. Squeege told
me he'd make sure things went good with Julie if I
did a few things to the school. I figured painting a
few signs was no big deal."

Kelly laughed then, but there wasn't much
humor in it. "Last night I phoned up Julie to brag
about what I'd done to the sign. She told me to
take a hike ... right after she told me about her
new boyfriend. He's twenty-four and a biker."
He took another breath. "I guess I'm pretty much
a joke right now."

"I don't think you're a joke," Pam said.

"Neither do I," Denny added. "By the way, you don't play football, do you?"

We all had a pretty good laugh at that, even Kelly. Trust Denny not to miss a chance to recruit a new guy.

Kelly looked at me. "By the way, Alex, I appreciate you going to bat for me when Denny was about to rearrange my brain cells. I guess I haven't been the greatest friend a guy could have."

"No worries," I said. "We'll call it even when we win the writing contest."

"Not a chance," Gail said. "My partner is Arlene Mitchell. She's an awesome writer. We're going to kick it!"

"Yeah?" I said. "Well, I've got a pretty awesome partner myself, and we're going to win. But don't worry, we'll still talk to you even after we're famous writers."

Actually we didn't win. When the results were announced the following week, Gail and Arlene did win, and we finished second. But the neat part was the judges said our two stories were so good, they were going to put both of them in the yearbook. I figured having my name in print right next to Gail's wasn't too bad.

15

It was time for the bull riding to start. I'd already explained to everyone how the event worked. Just like I'd done for all the other events. Expert, remember? Actually, Kelly sat with us for the first half of the rodeo, and corrected some of the stuff I didn't get quite right.

But now we could see him getting ready in chute number four. Everybody leaned forward except Arlene Mitchell. She put her hands over her eyes. "I don't think I can watch this," she said. But she did. She sort of peeked around Brad Murray's shoulder. The rest of us were really getting into it.

We cheered for everybody. Anybody who

gets on a ton of nastiness like a bucking bull deserves all the cheering they can get. So we cheered...loud.

The first two guys got bucked off in a hurry. Then a cowboy named Josh Douglas rode for the eight seconds. The announcer told the crowd Josh had a score of eighty-two points, enough to be in the lead. Then came two more buck-offs, and another successful ride—this one for seventy-eight points.

It was Kelly's turn. He was wrapping the tail of his bull rope around behind his wrist and into his hand. I knew that meant he was about ready to go. The bull he had drawn was named Ghost-buster. He was a big grey bull, with fair-sized horns. Ghostbuster stood fairly quietly. I figured that was a good thing, or Arlene might have had a heart attack.

I told everybody that this bull's normal pattern was to go out with two hard jumps, and then spin to the right. Gail asked me how I knew that. "That's what our business is—charting the patterns of the bulls, so the riders have at least a bit of an idea what to expect. And that's what this bull has done the last three times he's been out." What I didn't tell her was that the bull had bucked all three of those riders off.

"Our next cowboy is a talented young bull rider from Lawrence High School. In chute number four, it's Kelly Parker," the announcer said.

We cheered big time, even Arlene. Kelly nodded, and the gate swung open. Ghostbuster might have been quiet in the chute, but he was anything but quiet in the arena. He leaped high in the air, and came down hard on his front feet. Kelly got tipped a little to one side, and I was sure he was about to be bucked off. I figured out real quick that it was one thing to know what the bull might do, and something totally different to actually ride the bull while he did it.

Kelly somehow got himself back into the middle of the bull's back, just as Ghostbuster jumped, even higher this time. As his front feet hit the ground, the bull twisted and contorted his body, and then went into the spin to the right, just like my computer printout said he would. I couldn't believe an animal could spin that fast. Still Kelly sat there, his body kind of arched, and his free hand over his head to help him stay aboard.

And he did. All of us in the bleachers went nuts. In fact, I think the whole place did. When the announcer gave Kelly's score of eighty-five points, we all screamed some more. The next bull rider was bucked off, and the announcer told the crowd that Kelly Parker was the bull riding champion.

I took everyone down behind the chutes, and we pounded Kelly on the back to congratulate him. Well, the guys pounded—the girls hugged. I was starting to see the attraction of being a bull rider. That hugging thing was all right.

Actually, I was doing fine for hugs myself. As we stood there with Kelly and the others, Gail took my hand and gave it a squeeze. "That was cool how you knew what that bull was going to do."

"Yeah, well that's me, cool," I said, and everybody laughed.

"No, not just cool," Kelly laughed, "cowboy cool."

Denny groaned, and everybody else laughed

like crazy. It had been an awesome day. I had a feeling Shakey's was going to be a rockin' place that night.